Faggot

**FAGGOT: AN APPALACHIAN TALE
SURVIVING BULLYING**
By Frank E. Billingsley, PhD

Harvard Square Editions
New York
2015

Faggot

Copyright © 2015 Frank E. Billingsley

ISBN 978-1-941861-07-3

None of the material contained herein may
be reproduced or stored without permission
of the author under International and Pan-
American Copyright Conventions.

Published in the United States by
Harvard Square Editions
www.harvardsquareeditions.org

Dedication

This book is dedicated to all the people who had faith in me, just for being me, and not being something I am not.

Thanks, Melissa!

Preface

This book is about being different, about not fitting in, about the longing for acceptance. I have been writing this text, in my mind, for thirty years. Now is the time for me to tell my story. I tell it, not for me, but perhaps to save the life of a teen who is also lost in a society that gangs up on him or her. If I can help save one gay teen's life, if I can stop one person from suicide, I will have accomplished more than anything I have been able to accomplish in my past forty-eight years.

The time is now for gay people to take control of their paths and their destinies. It is time to stop permitting others to dictate who we are and who we should be! The time is now to be the author of our lives!

Table of Contents

Chapter 1: An Introduction

When most people reflect on their childhoods, they assimilate joy and fond memories of family and friends. Others recall a combination of happiness and heartbreak. The remainder, "the broken ones" look back and recall a horrific childhood. They feel fear, and they revisit psychological scars from their pasts. The scars that they carry are hidden deep inside their wounded psyches, the scars they wear into adulthood.

Humans are not civil by nature; we are often cruel and selfish. We reject what is different. We are fearful of things that we don't understand. Humans grapple with understanding differences; yet, it's individual differences that distinguish personalities and personae. In *Civilization and Its Discontents,* Sigmund Freud (1856-1939) said:

Men are not gentle, friendly creatures wishing for love, who simply defend themselves if they are attacked, but . . . a powerful measure of desire for aggressiveness has to be reckoned as part of their instinctual endowment. The result is that their neighbor is to them not only a possible helper or sexual object, but also a temptation to them to gratify their aggressiveness; to seize his possessions, to humiliate him, to cause him pain, to torture and to kill him.

Freud's view of human behavior resonates with how I perceive human nature. Humans obtain the undeniable desire to be aggressive and powerful as well as to objectify others. This I have experienced firsthand. I believe that this relates to the general idea that we are fearful of anything that we perceive to threaten our understanding of our world.

According to Velasquez (2005), "Human beings are so constituted that they must always act out of self-interest" (p. 75). This often occurs when we want to assert dominance, but this is also prevalent in adolescent behavior—more specifically, in adolescent males. This group inflicted much pain and suffering on me for nearly a decade. They exhibited torturous behavior because I was different, because I was not created to be part of the norm.

My individual difference is sexuality. Sexuality has divided humans throughout history. But in recent decades, there have been improvements in the understanding of sexual differences, and society shows more compassion, though the differences still remain. Variations continue to challenge humans and their fundamental belief systems and what they value as an acceptable human trait.

As an adolescent, when you are faced with the knowledge that you do not fit into the mold of acceptable human sexuality, internal strife begins. You are wounded and are emotionally destroyed.

It's difficult to find balance on how to fit into the acceptable norm. Recognizing that you don't fit within the norms leads to an emotionally stunted adolescence, which adds to the issues created by others who assert dominance over you. All this can create an even more confusing place to grow and develop. What I have described, thus far, is how I existed for nearly a decade: in a state of knowing that I was not normal and, further, knowing that everyone else knew that I was not normal. The issue of sexuality haunts me to this day, not because I'm not comfortable with myself, but because of the indignities inflicted on me as a child and adolescent.

There are many different beliefs when it comes to homosexuality. This book is not to give credence to homosexuality, but to raise awareness about the lack of humaneness that exists in society today. It has been historically proven that homosexuality has been around for as long as the Earth has been populated. It has been in fashion, gone out of fashion, and is what I would state at present as an ever-growing accessory.

Stories of torrid sexuality have been common from before Biblical times, extending from Asia, to the Middle East, and Europe. Although a book that was written over 3,500 years ago, *The Bible,* has dictated this mindset, many humans live by the words they choose appropriate for their lifestyles.

More recently, in the mid-twentieth century, "Sigmund Freud, who believed homosexuality development was neither a vice nor an illness, softened his views further by the end of his life. In 1935, a mother wrote to Freud for advice about dealing with her homosexual son" (Baldock, 2014, p.42); this is a significant statement that was overlooked by many psychiatrists and psychologists for decades, continuing the bondage of sexual expression.

I'm not writing this book to question whether homosexuality is a sin or an illness. However, it's my firm belief that homosexuality is not an abomination, but a naturally occurring trait. "Humanity" is a difficult word for Homo sapiens to understand. Is compassion a trait we are born with, or one that we learn? Many people, I believe, are born with the skills to comprehend and have the compassion to be caring and kind individuals. If they are born with this trait, they can grow to be kinder people through example and mimicking others in their environment. One must feel compassion to be able to offer compassion. One should not limit his or her humanity to something read in a book written centuries ago. Many believe they should live by the word of God, but sin the night before a service. They repent in church, but the fact that they carry hatred in their hearts limits their ability to offer compassion to others.

Ephesians 4:32 states, "Be kind to one another, tenderhearted, forgiving one another, as God in Christ forgave you." Man easily forgets this and attends church for salvation. Humanity has lost the ability to be compassionate when hate has entered the soul. People easily forget that the Lord also states in John 4:20, "If anyone says, 'I love God,' and hates his brother, he is a liar; for he who does not love his brother whom he has seen can't love God whom he has not seen." It's apparent to outsiders that modern people have forgotten what it means to be with God and that you need to love your neighbor, not wish to stone him for being outside your comfort zone.

There are many theories that relate back to why homosexual behavior has become part of our modern society. Homosexual behavior is traceable throughout our human past. Throughout most of our history, it has been a hidden form of sexual expression. Homosexual behavior and attraction exist throughout the world irregardless of our current political and religious leaders acknowledging or accepting it as a form of true sexuality. There is a lonely question: Has homosexuality increased as the population increased? Or has it always been around, and is it resurging, an event that has taken over 1,700 years to regain strength?

When did sexual behavior become a diabolical sin meriting death in many countries? For me, letting others live their lives is the basis of humanity. In my short life, I have had differing opinions of what constitutes good and decent human behavior. People are harmed physically and emotionally on a daily, if not hourly, basis. Why do we do this to our fellow humans? Over my years, I have seen one human inflict horrific acts on another. What I take issue with is, why are we so fearful of people who are different from us, and how can we permit abuse to occur continually?

There is an ongoing debate about why there are sexual differences. There are many hypotheses regarding the why and how. According to the cultural critic G. Roger Denson, one factor is "specifically the science and nature of population control, which makes homosexuality essential to the balance of life". This argument correlates with a Gallup poll from 2012, showing a steady increase in individuals who identify themselves as gay, lesbian, bisexual, or transgender (LGBT). The vast increase in homosexuality among the under-30 population is notable. The results reveal that the LGBT community represents only a total of 1.9% of the population over the age of 65, 2.6% among 50- to 64-year-olds, and 3.2% among 30- to 49-year-olds. More astonishingly, a large increase in homosexuality was reported among those under 30, doubling amount the people surveyed to 6.4%. Furthermore, regarding gender, those in the 18- to-29 age range, that is, 8.3% of women and 4.6% of men, identified themselves as LGBT (Rivera, 2012).

The United Nations (UN) recently released population projections based on data until 2012 and a Bayesian probabilistic methodology revealing that, contrary to previous projections, the world population is unlikely to stop growing this century, according to the Scientific American (2014). The United Nation suggests an increase of 57% to the prior estimated growth in the world's population. The new estimation will total approximately 11 billion people on our planet by 2100. One should question if homosexuality and the acceptance of the individuals, could indeed assist in the decreasing population. Can homosexuals, in fact, save the planet from an unsustainable future?

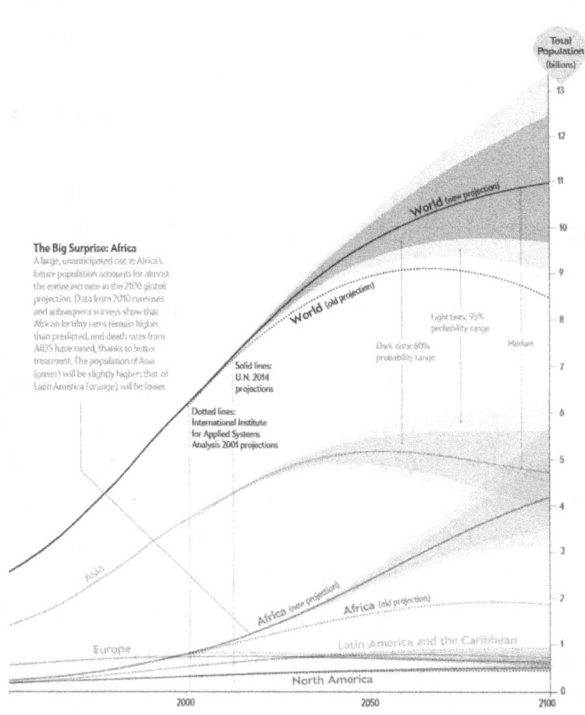

Hana Ševčíková and Jen Christiansen; SOURCES: "WORLD POPULATION STABILIZATION UNLIKELY THIS CENTURY," BY PATRICK GERLAND ET AL., IN SCIENCE EXPRESS.

Could this be a passable rationale for the causality of homosexuality? Could this be why LGBT individuals are becoming an increasingly visible part of our society. However, there is no solid evidence regarding the nature of sexuality. While it might provide a reason for people who need a passable rationale for sexual differences, to me, there isn't a need for a reason. Although the world is in the midst of a sexual revolution, people's attitudes remain volatile. Denson further illustrates, that nature is on the brink of collapse, due to overpopulation, and homosexuals are essential to the balance of nature.

The idea that Mother Nature in her wisdom has decided what is true and moral behavior could be an interesting argument for why homosexual behavior has become more prevalent in our modern society. The idea that Mother Nature has permitted same-sex couples to systematically assist Her in nurturing the numerous children that heterosexual couples were not able to raise could be Her ends to Her means. She, in Her majestic behavior, could be guiding Her world to a more sustainable future for those that continue to share Her world. In this case, sexuality could be the key to how our future world might sustain us.

The concept that my sexuality could be a key to the future stability of our planet actually gives me peace. I have a purpose. I believe that, throughout my childhood, I had a purpose in life, but somehow through the abuse that I had to endure, I lost that sense of purpose. Perhaps Mother Nature has always had a purpose for me. Although I have encountered some horrific people that have caused me great emotional harm, I feel blessed today that I have been able to be guided by my faith.

The horrific people I have encountered had no humaneness, but have blatantly disregarded other humans and the human condition. These are the types of people whom I'll be exploring in this book, the people who, out of fear, taunted, bullied, and tormented me for most of my childhood. Some of these individuals had been saved by the Lord, but don't ask for forgiveness for the pain that they inflicted on me, a human, that just happens to be gay.

I have not forgiven these people and have no innate desire to forgive them. The scars that they inflicted and the scars that humble me and made me the person I am today still burden me.

I'm not saying I believe that everyone from my childhood is malicious, but I can say with certainty that many people whom I have encountered are misguided and tormented souls. Did they enjoy tormenting me, did they enjoy belittling me, did they enjoy abusing me, did they understand what they were doing, where these behaviors natural to them? This, I can't answer. I don't know, nor will I ever know, why I was bullied and tormented during my childhood.

There are still young gay people in the world who feel they have no one to support them and turn to suicide, a tragic outcome. Over 30 years ago, the world was a different place, and suicide fits best in the past. The night that I feel I died was the night that I found myself. I understood who I was, and I know that I had a purpose. The goal of this book is to share my childhood experiences and to shed light on how bullying and being treated like a non-human changed my life. I often wonder, if I had not experienced this treatment, would I have turned out to be a different kind of human?

But did I turn out OK?

That, I can't answer. Do I, 30 years later, have fond memories of my childhood? My hometown? Or do I have contempt for the land that bore a man, a gay man, who still carries the scars and traumas of childhood?

Do I hate my history?

Do I hate the people I was forced to see every day? Honestly, I can't answer that, either. I have friends from childhood, long-lasting friendships. Others? I grow weak at the thought of their existence.

When I turned 18, I left New Lexington, Ohio (See map below from the Ohio Historical Center), for greener pastures (perhaps pinker pastures). For many years following, I'd go home for visits, driving down Route 13, past the old drive-in theater, down the hill into town…The hairs on the back of my neck would stand up, as if instinct were warning me of danger. Fight-or-flight mode would kick in, and I'd experience a tightening in the pit of my stomach. I wanted to throw up, or I'd experience the immediate urge for the nearest restroom. This feeling lasted for many years. I felt like an outsider—and still do.

New Lexington

Lake Erie

New Lexington

Ohio River

Did the torment that I received change my intended personal or professional development? On the contrary: I think that it helped me develop. Not necessarily because of the challenges and obstacles created, but because of the need to be successful, to be able to say that, regardless of what they did to me or what they said to me, I'd succeed. Their words won't hold me back. This still resonates in my mind, that I'm not less of a human.

The following chapters depict my experiences in a public school in the Appalachian foothills of southeastern Ohio. All the experiences I have chosen to share are true. There is no grandstanding; there is no creative license, only my experiences and my thoughts.

Chapter 2: A Reflection

Looking back, I realize I was a lonely child. That's an amazing thought, considering I'm the youngest of 11 children. However, with two to four years between all the siblings, my eldest sibling is 27 years older than I am. The family has grown over the years; I have over 50 nieces and nephews, and a recent promotion to Great-Great Uncle.

We didn't create a *Cheaper by the Dozen* home environment. Being born to parents later in life—my mom was 48 years old, and Dad was 50—didn't contribute to a traditional social life for a child. They were past the need and desire to rear another child, especially a child growing up in an ever-changing world.

Lonely is a very sad and isolated place. When you are forced to live in this state of mind, it stunts you, it limits you, and it hinders personal growth and development. It's a place of tears, a place of gloom, a dark place, and a place with the propensity to consume one's soul. Once you live there, it's a very difficult place to escape; it takes courage and tenacity. Alternatively, you must have the means to physically transplant yourself to a place where you can have a better mental disposition. But can you change your state of mind? Can you change your state of being? Can you learn to be less lonely? I can't answer that.

Loneliness is an old friend that leaves for long periods of time, but she returns as soon as she sees a vacancy notice. She knows how to take over with limited effort. She knows the exact places she needs to be to live and prosper. She lives rent-free while consuming her host. She has consumed me in many stages of my life; she often revisits. But I have always been able to evict her before she has consumed my soul. I don't know if she was always there or if she saw an opportunity in my despair and was able to take advantage of me. Was it my fault, was it genetics, or was she an opportunist feeding on the soul-destroying life I was forced to endure? I can't answer.

We lived in the Appalachian foothills of southern Ohio, about an hour's drive from West Virginia and Kentucky. The image below, from the Ohio Forestry Service, illustrates the view from anywhere in the region, and it shows a typical view of the countryside.

The main infrastructure was industry and coal mining. Manual labor was the key to life. My father was a coal miner for 39 years, spending eight to ten hours a day underground digging and ripping coal from the earth. He started working for a local coal mine when he was only 12 years old, tending the ponies that were used to pull the carts that brought the coal out of the mines: backbreaking work for all beasts involved. This work is hard on the body and mind, an endless day of darkness, heat, and coal dust that deadens the body's senses, beats one's spirit, and changes a person's disposition.

I remember being a child, playing in the deserted grounds of the place where my dad had worked. I remember the earth blackened from the remains of the coal scattered on the ground. I felt sorry for how the earth was left in such a state; no one cared enough to clean Her, to make Her beautiful again. She was like me, a product of the environment that was cast aside, discarded for everyone's viewing pleasure.

My dad's family members were all miners and hard workers. However, their one vice was that they liked to partake in the mass consumption of alcohol. I don't say this lightly: They were drinkers!

They liked their beer, their whiskey, and of course, their moonshine. They liked it, and they drank daily. My father included—he drank until 1958, when he almost sat directly on my infant sister. That was the end of his drinking—at least for the next 17 years, until he receive the calling again!

Mom was a mild, probably clinically depressed woman. She did what she could to make an end to a means. She was a hard worker. She didn't have the luxuries of life. She didn't have a new washing machine, "an automatic," until 1976. She washed our clothes in a wringer washer every Tuesday and Friday. For those of you that have not seen a wringer washer, it was a machine that had two rollers working together to "smooch" out the water in the clothes. It took hours on end to wash and rinse the clothes of six or seven people, let alone a coal miner's clothes!

The washing order was: whites, linens, towels, colors, jeans, and then work clothes, all in one tank of soapy water and rinse water. After this, the clothes went outside to the clothesline, where everything was hung individually with clothespins.

It's amazing to think that, considering she first moved to the house in 1939, she had been doing this same routine for nearly 40 years.

Were we poor? Yes, we were poor. We didn't have a great deal, not from fear of working, but because of the economy of the region. One thing we never went without was food, though; there was always an ample amount. My father ensured that we had a vast vegetable garden and various animals for butchering.

I remember my mother canning fruits and vegetables every summer to ensure that we had food throughout the winter months, including tomatoes, green beans, blackberries, raspberries, and a sundry of other vegetables. I recall our shed that was dedicated to storing potatoes and onions. And then there was the "meat shed," dedicated to the storage of meats. Autumn was a sad time, as we had to kill some of our animals to ensure that we had meat for the winter months. This was a horrific experience that left a long-lasting effect on my soul, standing for days cutting and grinding meat into steaks and hamburger. I blame this butchery for my lifelong vegetarianism and struggle with weight.

I remember childhood as a long time ago, although certain things I do remember with fondness, and some give me a little smile. One of those memories was how my sister and I would play with her Barbie's. There was one Christmas when my sister received the "Barbie Camper" and all the accessories. What a fabulous gift. I was so envious of her. I just wanted to play with that beautiful yellow camper van and dress Barbie in "high fashion." Yes, high fashion. Just because a girl is camping does not mean that she should look unkempt.

Then it was my turn, my turn, to open this big package! I slowly ripped away one piece of wrapping paper, then two, and I felt my face go numb. There it was in all its glory, my gift, my G.I. Joe camper van, big and green, with all the accessories, including G.I. Joe himself. I think it took a few more years to understand the value of his masculine appearance!

I remember all I wanted to do was to play with Barbie, and my sister was always accommodating and permitted me to play with her. This was a good memory, for not long after that, she became ill.

Our family was not greatly different from many families in the community, struggling to get by with what was available. Did this lack of material goods create harder workers or people who used and abused? It's my firm belief that all these factors contribute to being ill prepared to understand diverse human behavior, creating a platform for inequality, lack of self-acceptance, and lack of self-awareness.

I feel it's important to ask the question: if you work a great deal, does it deaden one's views of life? If you work manual jobs, do you lack the time to develop an understanding of others and value humanity for humanity?

There was a clear distinction between what is male and female, and if you didn't fit the stereotype, then you were labeled as different. Once you were labeled, it was virtually impossible to change your label.

Was I labeled? Yes, of course, I was labeled. I was singled out for abuse for nearly six years of my life, and it shaped and damaged my. These damages hindered my ability to trust, and they rendered me full of unsolicited anxiety and bouts of depression. These issues still exist, 30 years after I left a town that raised a gay man. I now tell you my story of how I was bullied for a decade. As I take you through my journey, I ask that you reflect on the prior discussion of why gay people are here. Do we have a purpose? Are we here as part of a bigger picture? A picture that Mother Nature, in Her divine wisdom, used as her brush to mark Her canvas with this diversified form of humanity? Take this journey with me; do not judge why I have finally put these words on paper. Do not judge why I reach out now. Do not judge me, for I am humanity at its best.

Chapter 3: Middle School

"Hey, faggot!"

"Hey, Faggot Frank!" I hear the words, but I ignore them.

"Faggot Frank!"

Smack! I feel a sharp slap on the back of the head.

"Hey, faggot, I'm talking to you." Smack, the back of my head burns as one of my tormentors continues to mock.

In the background, I can hear "a + b = c." At that exact moment in my life, I didn't care about whatever "a, b," or "c" meant. All I could think about was the bell ringing, giving me the opportunity to escape and be free of the embarrassing words that still resonate in my head.

All I wanted was the chance to walk through the sidewall. (I say, "walk through the sidewall," the classroom had a cubical shape this being a public school a design of the 1970s, that being Ohio, there was the belief that free-flowing knowledge was the key to the intellectual development of young minds).

"Faggot, don't ignore me!"

"Mr. Billingsley, do you want to share with the class?" I hear in the background. Mr. "Mathematics" was a middle-aged man, slender in build, I remember that he wore Cardigan sweaters and had a soft tone to his speak. Overall a very nice teacher with the patience of a saint. However, on that day he must've thought that I was causing the problem. I'm sure that he never heard me talk. I was afraid to answer questions; I was afraid to be singled out. I was afraid of being judged, I was afraid that I'd be hurt physically and most assuredly emotionally, and I was afraid they would laugh. I was afraid!

And how they would laugh at me for any utterance of a word. My normal response was, "I don't know!" This became a defense mechanism to protect me from the masses of people that physically, emotionally, and sexually abused me over the course of a ten-year period.

This is a stomach-turning thought, and I still become nervous when I have to speak in front of people. Today, I speak to large groups almost daily, and I still hold that innate, learned fear that I'll be laughed at. However, I have learned to cope with the distress and learn from my mistakes. This process was a struggle, and I have learned to use humor to deflect. A coping mechanism!

Smack. "Why weren't you in school last week, faggot? Where were you?" Again, another physical altercation from "Bobby". He was of an average build with dishwater blond hair, cute in a "hill-jack" sort of way. If I recall he wore a baseball cap and work boots everyday to school. I think this was out of "style" rather than necessity. He had a sarcastic demeanor, not quick witted, but surly in manner.

"I was sick with a stomach virus," I said, in hopes that this would divert attention from my absence. I looked at the ground, never in his eyes. If you look predators in their eyes, they will assuredly attack.

"Sick from what, faggot, sucking too many dicks? You like that, don't you, faggot?"

"You like to suck big, juicy dicks, don't you, faggot?"

"What a scum, you sick bastard."

These were some of the phrases and "cheerful jests" that would taunt me for the next few years. I say "cheerful jests" because when I'd have the courage to say something, I was told the kids were only teasing and that I should "man up."

It was the late '70s, the time of disco, the time of Little Debbie snack cakes. Little Debbie's are the best: sugar-coated sugar cakes, with sugar-cream filling, all the ingredients that any teenager wants in his or her staple diet. Donna Summers left her cake out in the rain, and disco was in. Disco was hot.

I was different, and everyone knew that fact. I didn't fit into this place. I hated my fellow students, I hated the teachers, and I hated the administrators. I was a target of abuse from the day that I took my first step into New Lexington

Middle School in August 1978. It was there as a venue of mockery and abuse.

Looking back, perhaps I can see why I was tormented. Image. I was around 5 foot 6 inches tall and weighed about 240 pounds. I had a 42-inch waist. I was effeminate and had Farrah Fawcett hair. Feathered! Can you imagine that we wore our hair like that? But we did. I was not attractive and often didn't have the best hygiene. I was depressed! I wore what my parents could afford, not the most stylish clothes, and not the best fitting, due to my size.

I went shopping one day for shoes at one of our local "boutiques." I do say "boutiques" in jest; I cannot recall what the name of the store was. You know, it was that store on the corner of Main Street and Brown Street. That store that all small towns have, the only place you really could buy any type of nice clothes. I was looking in the men's shoe department (Please take the word "department" with a grain of salt). The shoe department was what appeared to be an old closet that had the door removed. Then the strangest thing happened. The clerk in the shop was a young lady, very kind and sweet. She had a soft speaking tone to her voice; engaging though, she could draw you into a conversation with her consoling tone.

I hear, "That is all right, dear, I have big feet, too."

What was that supposed to mean? Was she implying that I looked like a young lady? Well, maybe I did look a little androgynous. I had larger hair, a nicely growing set of breasts, and a soft voice that had a hint of femininity. I am sure that I had not hit puberty yet; well, even when it hit, I am not sure it changed my appearance much. You see, I was not the typical overall- and baseball hat-wearing hill-jack. I was dressed in something straight off the rack from Rink's, a stellar department store that my family often frequented. You could buy anything, from animal feed to Jordache jeans. They had everything!

"I'll take a size 12, in those," I said. I was not ashamed that was my shoe size. Why should I be?

"Those look nice, sweetie—a nice, sensible shoe for a firm stride."

I'm not a horse, I thought, clip-clop-clip-clop!

"I think you will look nice in those. Do you have somewhere special you are going to?" Why should I answer her questions? Should I share my life with her, since she had no idea who I was?

One thing I forgot to mention was that my sister-in-law worked in the adjacent store. I had been in that store a hundred times, at the least. I guess that I was that unmemorable. I was forgettable. I was just someone that needed to buy shoes. This has stuck with me. Today, I have more shoes than most people I know. I love shoes: fun shoes, stylish shoes. I have no shoes for a good stride.

This was to become my life. I was the ultimate wallflower. This not out of choice, but out of necessity. I wanted to be the wallflower so no one would notice me. You see, this way I would be safe from them, from the ones that abused me.

No one really understood me. My teachers did not understand me. My peers did not understand me. My parents didn't understand me. I'm sure my family didn't understand me. In fact, no one actually took the time to try to understand me. Was this the reason that I was a target? Was this the reason I was sought out? Was I setting myself up to be a victim?

But, you see, I was not like them. I was not like the others in my community. I did not chew tobacco. Or use Copenhagen snuff. (On a side note, do you remember the round rings guys would have in their back pockets from sitting on the can of snuff for too long?). I didn't like to hunt. I didn't like cars. I didn't like motorbikes. I assuredly didn't want to talk about girls, at least in a typical adolescent way. I feel a little faint thinking about that!

I liked cooking. What? Boys don't cook, unless you aspire to be Emeril. I remember cooking and watching everything that my mother did in the kitchen. I remember her making pies. She would make six, seven, or eight pies at a time. She would make the crust for the pies, with some flour,

Crisco, and a little water. Her crust was always perfect. The one thing that I recall is that she never used a recipe. She estimated every ingredient, pinch, and stir. The crusts were always perfect. I enjoyed those times. It was a quiet time at home, and I was safe.

Although I was different, I must give my family credit. I have never heard a denigrating word from any of my siblings. They have never made me feel like I was inferior to them because of my sexuality. Do they agree with my life? I don't know, but they have never made me feel any different.

I set myself at a distance from them because I felt different. I was not worthy—a sick, sinister cycle that the mind created to ensure that I took on the blame, that I was the one at fault, that I was the freak that did not belong.

Chapter 4: Gym Class

Gym class. I still have an anxiety attack when these two words are spoken. I was tortured for 45 minutes every day for three years. I was emotional, physically, and sexually abused over a period of 45 minutes per day.

Fridays! They were the worst, dodge-ball day!

This game is a perverse process of half the class standing on one side of the gymnasium and the other half at the other end. The game starts when you throw thick, red plastic balls at each other until someone is the victor. Once you are hit, you then leave the game and stand alongside with raised, red welts. This was fun?

Seriously, what a traumatic game.

One of the "best times," I recall, was when the gym teacher left the area and one of my tormentors held up a ball and said, "Let's smear the queer. Come on, get him!" I remember at least 20 plastic balls bouncing off my head, back, and of course, my privates.

"Billingsley! You have got to learn to dodge" was the support that I received from my returning gym teacher. Coach was a middle-aged man on the heavyset side, and he always wore tracksuits and sweatpants. The typical look most physical education teachers strive for. Although, I think he was one of those tenure teachers who was just trying to complete his last few years of teaching before he could retire. Sort of a half-hearted teacher, but he did love his sports.

Dodge the balls? What did he say? Did he say, "dodge the balls"? How in the hell can I dodge balls if I'm surrounded 360 degrees? The words were there, but wouldn't come out: "Dodge this!"

I just lowered my head, ashamed.

Autumn was also a time for a "young homo" to be joyful in gym class: It was football season. And every red-blooded American wants to be the quarterback, but I always wanted to be a "tight end." I didn't know what that meant then, nor do I know what that means today—just a little fleeting "Mo" humor!

When the sun was shining, the boys were to play two-handed touch football. Everyone would change into some sort of hand-me-down gym clothes; sort of tarnished white colored shorts and tee shirt. Although we were playing two-hand touch, I often refer to it as "smear the queer" when the coach was not attentive. I can't remember the number of times that I found myself lying under a pile of adolescent boys. Oh, I remember, the pain associated with someone "accidentally" stepping on my head—or other vital organs.

"Billingsley! You have got to learn to throw the ball—not hold onto it."

Winter was the time for basketball. It was a poor school, so the easiest thing to do was to have the boy's strip down to demonstrate to which team they were assigned. This side, shirts, and that side, skins. This was the archaic practice of dividing the class into two. Regardless of where I was standing, I was always on the skins side.

"Hey, Billingsley, if you get any fatter, you'll

need a bra." The others would laugh. "Move it, fat ass. You're in my road."

"Hey, look. Faggot Frank is going to try to stop my layup ... ha ha." Slam! I feel my face sliding on the gym floor. Oh, how it burned.

"Billingsley! You need to watch what you're doing. You need to guard, not tackle."

Spring brought in a fresh scene, baseball season, and we returned outside to invest endless energy into hitting balls with bats.

Strike one!

Strike two!

Smack. I hit it, I hit the ball. What do I do? I thought, ah yes. I run to first base. I have to run. Run, you idiot!

I can't get my breath. How far away is that damn base? Ah, there it is, almost there. Slam! Why is my head sliding on the grass? Why am I on the ground?

"You stupid faggot, did you think you were going to make it to the base?" Hey, he tripped me. That asshole.

"Billingsley! Watch what you're doing. I don't

have time to take you to the doctor."

The whistle blows. Go get presentable. Oh no, I think today, I'll just wear my grass-stained shorts. I don't want to go into the locker room.

I pick myself up. Yes, I was on the ground again.

I'm the last one in the locker room. I see the other guys, very well-developed guys, just walking around.

Walking in and out of the shower, slapping each other on the ass with their wet towels. I go to my corner. I start to undress. ...

"Hey, faggot, stop staring at me."

"I see you looking at my dick. Do you like my dick?"

"I bet you have sucked dicks like this one. Do you want to suck it now?"

These comments come from one of my other enemies—I'll name him Billy (not his real name. Or is it? Do I owe any of these guys a favor?).

I just stare, thinking, Maybe I do—wrong answer. He stands there playing with his penis. Just stands there, playing with it. Is this really happening? Is he standing there, masturbating in the boys' locker room? He is!

"Hey, guys, look. Look at faggot Frank; he's staring at my dick.

"You little queer. Stop staring at me. You're giving me the creeps." He says this as he stands there with cock in hand—and I'm the "freak"?

I bend down to get my shoes out of my locker. Slap, something hit me in the face. He just smacked me with his dick. Did this just happen? I can't believe that he did that. He's hitting me in the face with his dick, and he's calling me the faggot.

Snap. What's on my head?

I'm amazed at the stupidity. Someone just put a jockstrap on my head. This is gross; it stinks. I sit there in fear, not knowing what to do. Fear of being hurt is worse than just emotional humiliation.

"Hey, look, faggot Frank is wearing my jock." The locker room full of naked guys is roaring with laughter. "You cock-sucking bastard."

I feel the tears welling up in my eyes. Stop. Do not let them see you cry. Stop! I feel a tear roll down my cheek.

"You little pansy....look at the little boy cry."

"Faggot Frank! Faggot Frank! Faggot Frank!"

The locker room roars.

I often reflect back on this situation wondering why he targeted me. Was he, in fact, gay? Was he trying to defend his dark closet? It is my understanding that he did get married and had children; but, a gold ring does not stop prying eyes and hands.

"Billingsley! How many times have I told you to stop wasting time and to get dressed? Why can all the other guys come in here, shower, and get dressed, and you are still in your gym clothes?"

Well, let me tell you why. I have had to watch a guy masturbating, and was forced to warn a jock strap on my head. That is why I'm not dressed, I thought to myself. I said, "Sorry, I'll try to do better." I felt like such an idiot.

Day after day, I saw his penis. He thrust it at me for the next two years. I was stunned—did no one ever see him? Did no one ever think this was odd? I did!

I didn't know what to do. You see, I was not a popular kid, and he was popular. He was on the football team. He was on the basketball team. He ran track. I was the fat faggot: There was no comparison on the popularity scale. Fear lived within me, and the fear of telling anyone was worse than living with the torment.

One day, I needed to go to the toilet; I was struck with an unnatural fear. One should not have a fear of voiding a bladder. But I had to go. I swallowed the lump in my throat and walked through the locker room. I could feel them looking at me. I walked. I went in through the sidewall (again, there are issues with doors in schools), and to my relief, no one was there. I let go and felt relief. Done and no one!

"Billingsley!" "Billingsley, who told you that you could use our toilet? Give me money for using it."

"I don't have any money."

"Then get down." I looked at him with a vacant gaze.

"I said, get down." I stood there vacantly.

I felt my arm-twisted behind my back, being pushed to the floor. My face was shoved into the urinal.

"Lick it. Lick it. If not, then lick the toilet."

"Lick it."

My heart was beating so fast in my chest; I could feel the blood emptying from my head. I did not know what to do.

"Why are you so mean to me?" Tears rolled down my cheek. "What did I ever do to you?"

"Shut up."

"Do what I tell you." I felt my hair being pulled back as he shoved his penis into my face. "You like that, little faggot, don't you? You like my cock, don't you? You like that, don't you, faggot Frank?" He rubbed it up and down my face.

This happened on a regular basis for years. No one cared. No one saw. How does one deal with this form of abuse? Perhaps in the '70s, no one knew. No one understood, but why me? Why was I the one who was tormented?

I recall one day when we finished class and were waiting for the bell to ring. We sat on the bleachers (we always sat on the bleachers). The coach had not come out of the locker room, and someone pulled me by the hair and dragged me over to "Bubba" a young guy on the heavier side, dressed in jeans, a tee shirt, and of course the ever popular baseball cap.

I found myself, again face down in his crotch.

"Look at the little faggot. He's giving Bubba head. Go on, faggot, suck it. Suck it."

"Billingsley, why are you on the floor? Why is there always something wrong with you? Get up."

No one cared. No one understood how this abuse was affecting me. My self-worth was being chipped away, day by day, little by little. I wanted to die. I had no reason to carry on.

Was this just a sampling of what my life was going to be like? Would I ever outgrow this? Was this just a phase in my life? Was this actually normal behavior and normal feelings?

These questions would remain unanswered for decades. Did this treatment lead to lifelong abuse and self-loathing behavior? It did result in a pattern of behavior that lasted for years, stifling my ability to trust others and my ability to grow as a person. I still hold remnants of these behaviors to this day.

All I thought about was ways to die. I began to imagine how I could end my life. Did I just want to take a bottle of pills, shoot myself, hang myself, or was that all a bit too dramatic? Should I accidentally hurt myself on the farm?

For the longest time, I lived in a diluted state—a state of fantasy, a state of clinical depression, a place where no one wants to live, a place where no one should have to live.

But I lived there. Today, my heart fills with sadness reminiscing over the years when I felt like I was inferior, that I was different, that I was odd, that I was a freak. Why me, out of billions of people in the world?

I'm sure that most people want to end their lives at some point, but I had this feeling for most of my adolescence. I wanted to die and end it. I'd show them what they did to me. I'd show them what they turned me into. Would they care then?

I know they would care; once I died, they would feel regret and know what they did to me. They would regret it the day that I died.

Chapter 5: Restroom Pen Ball

Buzz! A never-ending noise, until I turned the alarm clock off.

Oh, God, is it time to get up? It's now 5:30 in the morning, and I need to get moving before the school bus picks me up in 45 minutes for my hour commute to school. What an insane world! Who wants to be on a big yellow bus at that time of the morning? That's life in Appalachia. If you're not 16 and able to drive, then the big yellow bus is your method of transport.

Up! Straight into the kitchen to put on the coffee.

A girl must have her caffeine in the morning to be refreshed. Off to the shower, then dressed in some ridiculous Rinks' "prêt-à-porter." Back to the kitchen for my cup of coffee—milk and sugar, please!

I hear the bus coming over the hill. You see,

when you live in the country in the middle of a national forest, there is limited noise, and when I say, "limited noise," I mean you can hear the deer crossing the road.

The bus pulled up, turned around. I was the first stop. The doors opened, and I felt anxious, an unnatural fear of something to come. I got on the bus. We had assigned seats, and I was all the way in the back. All of the other kids were in the front. I think this was an isolation exercise for keeping the "mo" away from all the other children so they wouldn't catch it.

Off to school we went. We passed a grizzly bear of a man driving a big 4x4 truck with two rifles in the back window. No doubt just in case his first gun didn't work; he had a backup. I'm sure this happened often, just when you need a gun to shoot a fierce squirrel or rabbit. Oh, Lord. Here comes a second one and a third one. Perry County, Ohio, has kept the Dodge Company in business for the past few decades.

Anxiety! Oh, I can feel my heart racing. The bus stops, and he's not there. He didn't come to school today. The day has started well. The other person assigned to my seat was a popular guy—and one of the worst behaved. He used to get on the bus, and the first thing he did was punch my leg, my arm, my head … and of course, say, "Hey, faggot!" Then he and his friends would laugh, "Good one!"

Like I hadn't heard that before.

The thing that was the most annoying was when a guy would take his hand and cup it in a crescent or a circle and put it up to someone's mouth. Then he'd say, "Suck it." How they all laughed. Did people in other parts of the world make such jokes and then sit and laugh?

The bus approached the school, and all the kids would push to get off. The bus driver, looking on, saw nothing. We walked inside, and I needed to go to my locker. There was always someone in front of my locker. It was a daily ritual for me to get my books out. Then I'd finally get through the line of jokes and gestures—you know, the limp wrist signaling that I was gay. They were brilliant in their assessment. The one thing that those knuckleheaded jocks learned was to pick on a kid because maybe he was gay.

What they didn't know was that, at night, I used to have witchery parties. I used to write their names on a piece of paper, put it in a bowl, and pray to Mother Earth that they would stop bothering me. I took all the guys' names, put them in a cup, and then chanted,

"I ask upon Mother Earth to have these guys leave me alone. I ask upon Mother Earth to have these guys leave me alone."

I set the papers on fire. And now I can go to school in peace.

Faggot Frank! Faggot Frank! It echoes in my head. It never leaves. …

Now that I've made it through the locker gantlet,

I have a stack of books for five periods. You see, at this age, you can't be trusted to go to your locker between classes. You have to take all of your books for your morning periods. One would have thought that by lugging all those books around that I'd have lost some weight, but no, it made me want to eat more.

I made my way into the gym to wait for first period, while an inattentive teacher monitored the area. When you are in your teens, supervision was required, so in the morning you were permitted to sit in the cafeteria area or go to the gym. I normally sat in the cafeteria area ... alone.

But the day before had been a bad day of verbal torture. I decided that I'd try to hide somewhere alone in the bleachers. I was sitting there, minding my own business, reading a book—well, I think I was eating a Little Debbie snack cake—and Millie and Tillie (again, not their names, but fitting) came up to me and sat down. Why were these popular girls sitting with me?

"Hey, Frank. Do you masturbate?" I was shocked. Why did they want to know what I did in private? Before I realized what I had said, I said, "Yes."

Oh, dear Lord. What just came out of my mouth? I think I was imagining things—I really said "No." I did. I did. I did!

Regardless of how many times I said it, I knew that it was not true. "Where do you shoot?"

"In my hand!" I was on a roll. Think, man! I'm sure that, at that point, all three of our faces turned red.

What just happened here? Before first period, this personal information was shared with anyone that wanted to listen, and comments were made by all!

Why did I tell my intimate secrets to perfect strangers? Because I had no social skills. Growing up in the country, I talked to my cat and my pet cow Poop.

Yes, my pet-cow Poop. She was a beauty, a bright red-and-white Guernsey breed. She was like a pet dog. She was so tiny when my dad brought her home. She was too tiny to be put into the open field, so I fed her, brushed her, bathed her. … She was mine. My other friend was my cat, Felix. He was my best friend. He never judged me. He loved me unconditionally.

I loved riding my minibike, a 50. I used to ride

this bike from morning until night. You see, I pretended that I was a school bus driver for all of my friends. I had my route that I traveled twice a day to pick up everyone. I took them to their imaginary school, which was my house. In the day, it turned into a schoolhouse for about 15 kids—they were all my friends—there was Erica, Kiddy, Phil, Jesse, Steve, and only God knows the other names. I think there was a Mike, too. I had developed friendships with all the popular people at school in my imaginary world. I was very popular there.

I walk to the gym. I find a nice, quiet corner and sit there and watch the guys running up and down the gym. He has a nice ass in those jeans, I think to myself. If I had said this out loud, I would have been burnt at the stake, like a witch from Salem.

"Hey Frank, Frank! Come here."

I look up. Why is he talking to me? That's a popular guy. I say popular, because he was actually one of the nicer guys, perhaps he was used as pawn to lure in unsuspecting victims.

However, that aside, popular guys didn't talk to Faggot Frank! I think, Wow!

"Come here."

"OK!" My time has come. Will he ask me to sit with him and his friends? I get up to follow…and hesitate. Fear! "What do you want?"

"Come here. I want to show you something."

What would he have to show me? I don't even think that he's ever talked to me before. What's the harm? I pick up my books and follow. Because I'm a socially unskilled hillbilly, I follow him out of the gym, down that hall, and into the restroom.

I feel something on my back. Hey, he just pushed me … whoosh … slam right into someone else. Push … shove … push … shove. All my books go all over the restroom floor. I feel my eyes tearing up. Smash … I land on the floor.

"Score!"

"Smith gets 1,001 points for the high score in pinball!"

I was just made into the ball in a human pinball game. I look up from the floor, and I see six or eight guys lining the restroom walls, standing beside and across from each other.

"Look, Faggot Frank is crying. The little fucker is crying. Get up, you big baby. Get up." All I remember is that someone kicked me in the stomach.

"Don't tell anyone, or I'll kill you. Keep your fucking mouth shut."

I lay there on the urine-soaked floor of the boys' restroom. I lay there on the cold floor, not knowing what to do. I think this exact moment was the turning point. I sank into a deep depression. I felt lower than urine drops that I could see out of the corner of my eyes. Not one of the boys had any compassion for me. Not one asked if I needed help; not one helped me up. I feel a sharp pain, and someone steps on my hand and then kicks my books all over the restroom, each of my books soaking up the urine as they slide across the floor.

"Hello, Mom. I'm not feeling well. I just got sick in the restroom. Can you have Dad come and get me?

… Yes, I just threw up."

What I want to say is, "Hey, Mom, I was just kicked and physically assaulted in the restroom by eight guys." That is what really made me sick, my nerves! I had a weak constitution for a 13-year-old.

"Frank, Frank! You're going to miss the bus."

"Mom, I don't feel good. My stomach's aching. I can't go to school."

This was the start of my missing nearly two months of school. The thought of going back sickened me. I was finally away from them. In my head, this was the solution. To the school administrators, it was a different story. The school filed truancy charges against my parents, and we had to go to court. Not one time during this process did anyone ask, "Frank, are you OK?"

The system let me down. There was no intervention. No one offered to protect me. No one offered to make things right. I remember that, during this time, I'd lie in my bed for half the day. I didn't move. And when I did move, it was to eat and eat and eat. I ate everything in sight. To this day, I still eat when I'm depressed, anxious, nervous, and in pain. Food comforts me. It comforted me then, and it comforts me today.

"Hello, hello, operator, can you give me the number for any private schools in the Columbus area?"

"No, I need to have a name to help you."

"Are you sure I just need the name of one school?"

"Sorry, I'm unable to assist you."

I had a big plan to leave home and go someplace better, someplace where I wouldn't be bullied ... someplace far away. I never wanted to go back. I was finally out of there.

I knew that, if I didn't find a solution, I'd have to go back. I did everything that I could think of, and nothing was available. There was no one there to help me. I was alone in my strange, little world. I'd never be normal. And if I had to go back, I knew that would be the end of me. I wouldn't make it. I'd finally have to kill myself, or the bullies would finally push me over the edge. I'd be sent to the psych unit, the locked unit at Bethesda Hospital. No one wanted to go there. I didn't even want to go there, because they would find out my secret, that I was gay. That would be worse than being tortured.

Being gay was one of the worst things that anyone could possibly be in those days. If you were gay, you would assuredly already have GRID (Gay-Related-Immune-Deficiency). This was the terminology used when AIDS was only associated with the gay population. I was bound to die anyway, so suicide would end it all before I had to go back to school or admit that I was gay.

My mother received a telephone call from the doctor. I had been to his office a multitude of times, and finally, they found out that I was destroying myself from within.

"Mrs. Billingsley, he has a peptic ulcer."

"Is that normal for a 13-year-old?"

"No, this is not normal for a 13-year-old. But he'll be fine. He'll have to take some medicine for a while."

My nerves had gotten the best of me. I was on a spiral. "I think Frank needs to go and talk to someone. I think he has some issues."

Listen Doc; I have no issues, except for the assholes at school that pick on me.

Well that could be part of it, for you see, when I was eight, my sister died. She had cancer. She died when she was only twelve and I was only seven. I remember us a year before playing with her Barbie's and the camper van. What a wonderful memory. I wondered how my life would have been different if she had lived.

Would I be like I am? Would I be as fat as I was? Would I be a sissy? Would she have protected me? I'll never know. After she left us behind, I withdrew from the functional world.

In addition to that baggage, my father had started to drink again. He drank about a bottle of whiskey a day. Life was not good. My father was a verbally violent alcoholic that gradually turned physical. He used to say nasty things to my mom. He hated me, and I hated him.... Why was I here?... I was adopted.... I was just given to my parents…. I didn't belong to them.

Yes, I did. I was theirs for good or bad. Times were not all bad. We had some fun times, in between Dad's stints in rehab and Mom's stints in and out of the hospital. She had rheumatoid arthritis, and it was very debilitating. She ended up bedridden and died when I was just 20.

I finally was picked up from school, and I went straight to my bed. I felt numb; I no longer felt human. It was time to take the pills. Life was far too complicated, and I did not understand it. What a sad mess I was in.

Chapter 6: Study Hall

For those who don't know what study hall is, it's a free period, a time during the normal school day when students can complete their homework assignments—a brilliant philosophy. But what was mostly overlooked was that, in a study period, kids need silence and to be supervised.

Our study hall was not in a beautiful library, but in a strange and precarious place. Our study hall was in our school cafeteria, a general, all-purpose area that was utilized for lunch, school dances, and even choral productions. Our cafetorium had a stage. This stage served as a perch for the study hall teacher, the supervisor of the students therein.

In my eighth-grade year, I remember having Mrs. E. She was a petite, rotund lady of retirement age, if not long past the expiration date. She was not fragile, but a lady who had spent the past 40 years teaching middle-school English. She wore muumuu dresses that made her look as broad as she was tall.

She was shrill in her demeanor and yelled more than she talked to all in her presence. The issue was, she had no control of her 40-odd students—"odd" meaning give or take, although there were a few odd characters in the hall. The guys that used to pick on me also picked on her. They would tease her to get her agitated.

"You boys have no respect for anyone. You mark my word, this will come back to you." These memories still resonate. I often wonder if karma ever visited those guys.

"Hey, Billingsley—faggot, if you don't answer me, I'll fuck you up," one or the other would scream.

"What? Just leave me alone."

"Fuck off, you little faggot."

"Billingsley, when was the last time that you sucked a cock? I bet you love cock in your mouth. Why don't you get under the table and suck me now? Better yet, I have to take a piss. Open up."

I sat there in fear and fright. What was I supposed to do? How do you respond to this? How do you expel the sick feeling in your stomach? How can you stop gazing at the floor? How can you hold your head up and feel like a human? I think that what people don't realize is that, with continual degradation, you lose the feeling of being human.

This verbal abuse continued daily in this setting. For a thirteen-year-old who is already sexually confused, abusers cause extreme damage to an ego.

Looking back, there were days when I wanted it all to end. I wanted it all over. I remember one day that was exceptionally bad, when the girls got in on the taunting. The girls were "Candi, Mandi, and Billy Jean"! Fictitious names, offering a hillbilly flare. They were the typical looking 80"s teenager. Big hair, curls, and did I mention BIG hair. I am sure they were wearing some fashion from the discount store in New Lexington. I cannot remember the name? Tee-Jays, I think we called it "Tiggies", the "high quality" department store!

"Frank do you masturbate?"

"I bet you eat your own sperm." Ha ha … ha … I hear them all laugh.

"Billingsley eats his sperm."

"You eat yours, but you won't even suck me?"

"Faggot!"

Today was the day. Today, I will end it all. I can't come back here tomorrow. I can't, I can't. I hate it here; I hate all of them. I feel the tears rolling down my face. I see their faces laughing at me. I feel warm, like I'm going to pass out.

The bell rings, and I go to the bus to go home. I think this day was just one of those bad days. The bus was just one bully after another. It was like going through an obstacle course, of verbal abuse, punching, and tripping. Didn't anyone see? Did no one hear? Today was the day, the day to pass over. I arrive home. I have been collecting pills, and I have a stockpile. When do I do it?

I'll do it tonight before bed. I'll simply go to sleep, and then I'll never have to wake up again.

My days of torment will be over. I won't have to face those people again. I'll never have to hear, "It's just teasing. You need to get over it."

At bedtime, I notice that my Mom is not feeling well. I note she is having problems tonight. You see, my Mom has been struggling for many years. Mom is now on her way to the hospital, and I'm in even more distress because today is not the day I'll die.

Since Mom is in the hospital, I don't have to go to school the next day. I have a day of reprieve. I lay there, gazing at my pictures of Shaun and David Cassidy, which I had plastered all over my bedroom walls. ... I liked their music. ... No, I thought that they were hot!

Chapter 7: The Dinner Bell

In the '80s, if there was a "the" place to be and be seen in New Lexington, Ohio, it was the Dinner Bell. To begin, let me set the ambiance of the establishment—it was a house turned into a restaurant, a large Victorian-ish house that had an extension built on it to establish the fact the building was an establishment, not a house. There was a wood porch built in a wraparound manner.... This was the place where everyone would hang out. If you were cool, you needed to be seen there. It was a pizza place-cum-sub shop, which for some reason became a hangout for the teens of the community.

Where can one begin to describe the desire to be there, to be part of the cool crowd ... but secretly knowing that I'd never fit into the "community," the tribe?

Why did my moped break down here, in front of

the Dinner Bell? Dear God, I have to go inside and use the phone. The thought of this nauseates me, and I can't breathe. My heart is pounding in my chest; it's going to jump out.

I slowly look left and right to see who is around, and the coast appears to be clear. I walk carefully across the street. Seeing the pay phone on the porch, I call Dad, asking if he can come and help me.

"OK, OK. I'll be there soon."

"Frank? Come have a Coke with me." I look in the window, and it appears to be safe. One of the popular girls has asked me to have a Coke with her. "Hi, can I have two Cokes, please?"

"Sure, I'll bring them right over," Mrs. Daugherty says. We sit down in one of the booths. Someone is playing pinball in the background. Ding, ding, ding, went the game. Mabel and I sit there and talk about the upcoming play; I think that it was Li'l Abner. Mabel was a nice girl, funny, laid back, but she had a brother who was the spawn of Satin!

Then to my embarrassment, "Mabel, what are

you doing with that faggot? Get your ass home. And you, get the hell away from my sister."

I could feel the fire burning up my neck, the pulsation of fear in my face; I know that it was beet red; I was so embarrassed. I either wanted to cry or crawl under the booth.

I note that Mabel, too, is beet-red with embarrassment. She is embarrassed to be his sister, or at least, that is what I choose to believe. Do I know this as a fact? No, but in my heart, I do want to believe it. I want to believe in the human soul, that people are not cruel by nature. She was truly embarrassed, but after all, I think she was embarrassed for herself, not for me. She was red-faced from her own discomfort, not for my deep sadness and fear.

I was always afraid in these situations. Even writing these words now, I feel the sensation burning in the pit of my stomach. Why do we hold on to that feeling, that feeling of being ashamed?

I was frozen. I couldn't move, and I couldn't respond. Was I safe? Was I going to be hurt? Or would I be publicly humiliated yet again? That's the one ... humiliation.

"Humiliation" is a term that resonates throughout my teen years. What is humiliation? What does it mean to me? It signifies the multiple occurrences in my adolescence when I was made to feel sub-human. How can words and actions beat someone down so far that they don't feel human? But are we human, or are we part of something bigger? Or are some of us human, and others, not? Is there a fine line that defines what makes us human? If we do not fit into a mold, are we indeed not human? If someone is cruel, in my view, I do feel that person lacks humanity.

Remarkable or not, we are all, indeed, human by nature. But to define "humanity" is different. Humanity is marred with deviations from and derivations of what we were created to be, whether from a divine creator or through genetic evolution. But, whatever you believe, there is no excuse for being hateful or harmful to other human beings.

I do believe my peers didn't know better. Was the cause for their abuse the culture in which I grew up, or was it the hatred and misunderstanding of anyone different from the norm? But what is the norm, and how can a small town in southern Ohio dictate the norm? Were these people lost souls? Had they experienced something similar? All I know is, I didn't fit in, and I didn't belong.

How do you recover from a bad situation? You ignore it. "Well, Frank, it was nice talking, but I should be heading home for dinner. I hope your Dad arrives soon."

Hey? "Bye!"

I exited as fast as I could. I sat in the car.

Chapter 8: Football Games

Do you remember high school Friday night football games? For the majority of the population, a lively football match is the ending to a long week.

The Panthers were revered and feared. However, I feared them in a very different way. You see, the majority of the team had at one point belittled me, put me down, and physically harmed me in sundry demeaning and cruel ways.

So, why would I go?

Because that is what you did in Appalachia. You went to football games on Friday nights. There was no reason to fear. There were adults there; someone would look out for me. I could stay close to the bleachers.

The bleachers were filled with cheering fans, supporters of the team. They would yell and scream for the team, and on occasion, they'd jeer at the passersby.

Imagine a standard football field, surrounded by a track with opposite ends occupied with bleachers for the home team and the guests. What the young people would do was to walk around the track.

The track was a minefield of ill-behaved youths that were up to no good, out of the prying eyes of adult supervision. On the track, the abuse started, one ill-begotten night. I was on the left-hand side of the bleachers, near the cheerleaders, standing on the track, alone, minding my own business.

As I said, I was a very unpopular child, the person or nonperson that people would overlook the majority of the time. But when someone needed to feel superior about themselves, I was the target, satisfying their need to fill their bodies with adrenaline.

On an average night, there would be hundreds of people at the football game. Then, with a few hundred kids walking around the track, it would get crowded. Sometimes, suffocatingly crowded. There would be bottlenecks in the flow of people to get through some areas, such as where the cheerleaders would be putting on a show. "Go, fight, win!" Or some such cheer to encourage fans to rally around the players.

Smack, my shoulder was hit so hard, I lost my balance. The next thing I knew, I was on the ground. I think one of the players had mistaken me for the opposing team. Is that possible? Wait a minute. I'm on the track. Why are people looking at me? I feel a bit confused. Why is no one helping me up? I see in the distance three, maybe four guys laughing. Then I see another group of guys laughing.

I realize I'm still sitting in the dirt and people are just walking on past, ignoring me. Was I really there? Was I dreaming this? Why wasn't anyone helping me?

"Ha, ha. Look at faggot Frank. In the dirt where you belong." "Don't cry." "Oh, my God, he is going to cry." "What a little faggot."

I feel water on my face, but I'm not crying. I'm afraid to cry. Wait! I can't believe it. Is it raining out?

Where is this water coming from? Is it raining? Is someone throwing water on me? I feel a sinking feeling in my stomach. They are. They are: They are spitting on me.

I'm sitting here, surrounded by hundreds of people.

People are passing by, and no one notices me. No one has even noticed that I'm sitting in a crowd of people, and five, six, seven guys are spitting on me. I see the crowd getting larger. They are all looking at me, but no one is helping me. I'm still sitting there in the dirt, covered with spit and the smell of chewing tobacco. All I know is that it smells. I hear the laughter increasing. I know now they have taken my last shred of human dignity. It has been taken.

I stand. I now have to walk through the crowd covered in human fluids. I feel so violated. I feel like the dirt that I was sitting in. I walk toward the restrooms. I see out of the corner of my eye that someone is following me. No, I'm being paranoid. As I indicated before, fight or flight, but for me, it was always flight.

I go inside, safe; there are adults inside. "Son, what happened to you?"

"Nothing," I reply. No one is concerned, no one was moved, no one knew who I was.

I go to the sink and begin to wash off the remains of the human fluids that violated me.

I feel my arm in pain. What the hell? Someone is pulling me. I resist, but I'm tired. I'm weak from the experience. I'm then dragged into the stall. I'm pushed on the toilet, and someone is standing over me. I can't see his face. There is a light. I can't see well. However, I see it. I see a penis. He is holding it. He is masturbating. He masturbates faster and faster. I try to move. He's pushing me down, standing over me. He pins me against the toilet. I hear a moan, and I feel warm fluid on my face. This went on for what felt like an eternity, but in reality, it only lasted for a few minutes.

"Look what you made me do, you stupid faggot. You like my cum, don't you? If you tell anyone, I'll kill you." Until someone states those words to you—"I'll kill you"—you don't understand the fear, associated with years of abuse. I'm still unclear about who this was, but the fear and shame still reside in my psyche.

I wanted to die. I didn't want to live this life anymore. I didn't want to have to experience this ever again. He left, and I cry, I sob. I'm alone in a filthy toilet, covered in spit and semen. I'm a toilet for the world. I do my best to clean up. I make my way to my moped, and I go home. I feel sick.

It has taken me 30 years to finally talk about this belittling abuse. I still feel shame about this abuse. I carry the guilt. In reflection, I wonder if this was someone I knew, was it one of the boys from my gym class? If I were to answer this honestly, I did not recognize the voice, and he seemed to be a mature man. He could have been anyone; he could have been a victim, like me, who turned into an abuser. I feared that he had been stalking me; he saw me being victimized and realized that I was a victim he could use me. Was he in fact gay, or was he only after the control of harming someone. These questions I can only speculate, and only hypothesis to why he abused me. Either way he knows who he is and perhaps he will come forth.

Chapter 9: The Day That I Died

The football game was on Friday night, and I had a long weekend to ponder over this latest incident. However, I was numb most of those 48 hours. I do not remember thinking, I do not remember feeling, I do not remember a great deal of the occurrences that weekend. I recollect being in my bedroom, and staring at the white swirled ceiling, but not feeling anything that would indicate brain functioning.

I hear that sound, buzz!!!

I recollect waking up on that Monday morning. I'm not going to school. ... I don't have the strength. I don't have the mental faculties to get up to get dressed. ... I'm so sad, I'm so unmotivated, I can't move. I was so deep into a pit; I couldn't see a way out. ... Most people see a light at the end; I see a curving pit ... an endless winding tunnel! I can never, ever get out of this hole.

Mom entered. "Time for the bus." Almost intuitively, she knew I was not going to school. I got up and got ready.

I see the bus. I hated the color yellow then, and now, every time I see a yellow school bus, I sense a fear of my past. I get on the bus, and all is fine for the first 30 minutes. Then the bus stop is approaching. They all get on and start with, "Faggot Frank, faggot Frank," smack! A smack upside the head, but the sharpness was gone. I didn't feel the pain. The feeling of pain had left my body. I no longer feared them. I was just there. I was existing, but not alive.

My mind became distorted. I lost hope. I felt so degraded that I felt nothing. I felt worthless. I didn't want to live. I felt like I actually deserved to die.

When you finally reach that place, that place of the darkest day of your life, the day you know will be your last; there is a feeling of numbness, a feeling of going through the motions, but yet not understanding the ramifications.

Looking back now, the day I planned to die was not about me, but about them. I was depressed, unhappy, and hated everything because I was told that I was a fat, little fairy-bastard-faggot. I let myself believe that I was all of these things, because the "cool" kids told me so. They were the "cool" kids, so they were right.

I had no reason to live.

The day was unmentionable: same day, same shit, and same abuse. But I had a secret that gave me the strength to get through the day.

This was the day that I'd do it; I would end it all; this was the day that I would die!

I won't have to see those people again. I'll never be attacked … never hit … never slapped … never called an abusive name. I'll be free from this hell that I have called my life. It was a dark, October day. It was grey; the leaves were in full autumn color. It was a cold, rainy day.

What a perfect day to die.

I said goodbye to the world, goodbye to a miserable existence, goodbye to my life of misery!

The day ended. I said nothing to anyone. I went to my room in darkness and silence. I get my stash of pills…. I grab the bottles…. I take a handful. ... I swallow them all. ... I can't describe the relief. I let it all go, I let the hate go, I let the fear go, I let the anger go, I let the contempt for mankind go. I lay there, settling into a warm bed and thinking I'll no longer have to go back to that jail, or asylum, that school

I start to think of all the hateful things that had been done to me in the small Perry County town, the town that had created a generation of racist homophobes. In the course of three years, I was tortured for 180 days per year. There was not a day that went by when I was not taunted—hit, had books slapped out of my hands, was shoved on the toilet floor, had food thrown at me, had my things stolen, had a penis shoved into my face, and endured daily bouts of physical abuse, daily emotional torture, and sexual abuse.

Why me?

What had I done to any of them? What had I done to deserve this treatment? Ah, yes, I know now. I was "different," and everyone knows that when someone is different from the norm, then one deserves to be beaten, broken, and thrown by the side of the road.

I sob for what I recall was hours upon hours. I cry over the emotional abuse. I cry over the physical abuse. I cry over the sexual abuse. I let it go. I feel cleansed. I feel like a weight has been lifted. I am at peace.

The next thing I remember, I gasp for air, and I see darkness! Not just dark—but darkness that was so deep that it equals the doom you feel in your heart.

I'm awake. … What time is it? Wait, I'm not supposed to be awake. I'm not supposed to be alive! It's the middle of the night, 3:09 AM, when I realize I am alive.

I remember the fear that I still held inside me paralyzed me. I lay there staring at the ceiling, not knowing what to do, not knowing if I should try to take more pills, or whether I should take it to another level and use other means to end my shattered existence. For some reason, Mother Nature gave me a boost of energy and moved me out of my bed.

One would want that day to have a fairytale ending; however, the day ended up being yet another day of verbal and physical abuse. What I learned was that I was a survivor. I needed to remind myself that I was a fighter, not necessarily a fighter in the sense of protecting myself, but in the sense of having an innate need to survive.

I sobbed until morning. I was so useless that I couldn't even kill myself. As I lay there, I tried to figure out why I lived. Why was I still alive?

This moment, I'll remember the rest of my life.

This was the day that I was supposed to die, but looking back now, it was the day that I died. The person I was had died on that cold and rainy night. The darkness had lifted; I realized that I needed to work on me. Try not to be the victim. I rationalize that I was as important as all the others. And I knew that suicide was not the answer. I acted like a victim, and I was treated like a victim.

On that day, as I said, a part of me died, and I had to rethink my existence. The day I awoke and realized that I had not died was in itself a tragic experience. Mother Nature had molded me for a reason. She gave me the strength to survive. She gave me the strength to move forward, and She gave me the guidance to have a desire to help others. I feel that my existence has assisted in helping our world to be more sustainable.

It was now time for school. I had to get up and get ready. Did I have the strength to make it, to go back, to face these people? I had no choice. Mother Nature decided that I need to be here for a reason. I have a purpose in this world, and now I must live to ensure that my purpose is defined and that I have a destiny.

In the days to come, I did not have the courage to tell anyone that I was gay. If you remember, I said that fear was an old friend, and she was still there even in my hours of growth. Although, I was unable to share the true me, I did the next best thing. I joined "The Drama Club" and became a "thespian". From this experience, I was able to use my attributes to the fullest and make people laugh!

Chapter 10: Understanding the Outcomes

I didn't die. I can say now that I'm happy that I didn't die, but the road that one travels as an adolescent is a hard one. The abuse didn't stop the next day, the next week, or even the next few years. Things became better, but they didn't improve because of that night. I do believe that a part of me did die that night. Perhaps there was a part of me that needed to die to ensure that I grew into the person I am today.

Did I change that day? I again can't answer that. Nor can I say that the scars healed. Did I repress them so deeply in my psyche that I'm unable to retrieve them? Regardless, I do feel that I gained strength on the day I wanted to die. And it did change my life. I'm not condoning my behavior, and I don't wish these actions upon anyone. Nor should anyone follow my example. I changed because I had the strength to change. I had let go of all the hate and fear. By doing this, I was able to free space for my personal growth.

I don't know where I pulled the strength from, but perhaps Mother Earth heard my prayers. Perhaps she gave me the strength to wake up and start a slow process of change.

For me, there are still many unanswered questions. Why me? Why was I an outsider in the tribe? Why was I pinpointed for abuse? Was I a victim? Once you have been exposed to these types of traumas, can your psyche rebound? Does this create patterns of behaviors?

Why me? This is a question that I know will never be answered. I was weak, and being weak, I opened myself up to abuse. It does not make it right, but it's a good sign of growth when you can acknowledge that you don't know. You become fine with that.

Why was I an outsider in the tribe? I was the anti-tribe. I was the total opposite of the perfect Appalachian guy.

Why was I pinpointed for abuse? This, too, can't be answered, but I don't want to answer this.

I don't want to know. It happened. I have dealt with it, and I have moved on. This progression lives in my adult persona.

Was I a victim? I was a victim. I was a victim because I was what my abusers considered abnormal. Once you have been exposed to these types of traumas, can your psyche rebound? Yes, you can rebound. Within each of us, we can rebound and become even stronger. We must believe in ourselves. Once we can believe in ourselves, we can gain strength to succeed.

Does this create patterns of behavior? Yes, it can. I do think that I have fallen into this pattern. I needed to fix things. Problems. People. I needed to help myself and others. I do believe that this behavior pattern has guided me into the professions of social work and education.

I do believe that I died that day. A small piece of me withered away. But I have to say that I'm happy that I didn't die that day. I have had so much to offer this world by being alive. Through my work, I have saved children from abuse, helped adults with psychoses, helped treat substance abusers, and educated an international audience. If I had died that day, I'd have no legacy to share. It's my hope that my words can save a child in similar situations.

I often wonder where these people who abused me are now. What has become of their lives? What I can gather is that a large majority of them still live in the town that tormented me for far too long. They have married, had children, and have productive lives. But, why? Is the old adage, we were all "kids" a valid excuse? What I hope is that they have taught their children to be better humans than their parents taught them to be. I can only ask!

My life has led me in many directions. I have lived in Europe, and traveled the world. I completed college with a degree in psychology; I have two masters' degrees in human ecology and management, and I have a Ph.D. in leadership and administration. I was a social worker for many years saving children from abuse and neglect. I worked in a mental health facility. I am teacher. I am an administrator. And I am a professor. But, one thing that I am and I always will be is a gay human being. I am not ashamed; nor am I embarrassed. I will not hide who I am; nor will I change who I am. I want to let the younger generation know that being gay is not a life sentence. Whatever is happening to you now can change and will change. Please give it time to change. You will become the author of your life.

It's important never to tell your child to "man up." Always listen to everything that your child tells you. Create a "bully-free" zone in all aspects of your child's life. It's important to note that we humans can still continue to coexist with tolerance.

I encourage anyone that is living in fear to reach out to someone, talk to someone. There is no reason to be fearful of being gay. I encourage you to come out and embrace the life that is waiting for you. Don't be a victim any longer by hiding in the dark places of your closet and the closet minds of people around you.

Embrace the life that is to come!

Sources

Scientific American. (November 18, 2014). World population will soar higher than predicted, http://www.scientificamerican.com/article/world-population-will-soar-higher-than-predicted/ reprinted from Hana Ševčíková and Jen Christiansen; SOURCES: "WORLD POPULATION STABILIZATION UNLIKELY THIS CENTURY," BY PATRICK GERLAND ET AL., IN SCIENCE EXPRESS. PUBLISHED ONLINE SEPTEMBER 18, 2014 (2014 projections); "THE END OF WORLD POPULATION GROWTH," BY WOLFGANG LUTZ ET AL., IN NATURE, VOL. 412; AUGUST 2, 2001 (2001 projections)

The Bible. (1985). New York: Doubleday.

Baldock, K. (2014). Walking the bridgeless canyon. Reno: Canyon Walker Press.

Denson, G.R. (2010). Homosexuality as population control? Why gays & lesbians are essential to the balance of nature. Retrieved from http://www.huffingtonpost.com/g-roger-denson/is-homosexuality-populati_b_784449.html

Freud, S. (2010). Civilization and Its Discontents. Eastford, CT: Martino Publications.

Forestry Service. (2014). Retrieved from http://www.fs.usda.gov/Internet/FSE_MEDIA/stelprdb5438732.jpg

Ohio Historical Central. (2014). Retrieved from http://www.ohiohistorycentral.org/images/0/04/New_Lexington_map.jpg

Rivera, J. (2012). New poll shows more young, poor people of color identify as LGBT. Retrieved from http://colorlines.com/archives/2012/10/more_than_half_of_latinos_say_they_favor_allowing_gays_and_lesbians_to_legally_marry.html

Velasquez, M. (2005). Philosophy: A Text with Readings. Boston: Cengage

More books from Harvard Square Editions